A. J. Bryan

Architectural Proportion

a new system of proportion showing the relation between an order of

architecture and a building of any kind

A. J. Bryan

Architectural Proportion
a new system of proportion showing the relation between an order of architecture and a building of any kind

ISBN/EAN: 9783337387426

Printed in Europe, USA, Canada, Australia, Japan

Cover: Foto ©Andreas Hilbeck / pixelio.de

More available books at **www.hansebooks.com**

A NEW SYSTEM OF PROPORTION SHOWING THE RELATION BETWEEN AN ORDER OF ARCHITECTURE AND A BUILDING OF ANY KIND.

RULES FOR FINDING THE HEIGHT OF FOUNDATIONS, BASES, WATER-TABLES, WINDOW
SILLS, DOORS, WINDOWS, BALUSTRADES, AND SUPERIMPOSED STORIES; WIDTH
OF DOORS, WINDOWS, ARCHITRAVES, PILASTERS AND POSTS; HEIGHT AND
PROJECTION OF ENTABLATURES, CORNICES, AND ALL EXTERIOR
FINISH; ALSO HEIGHT OF BASES, WINDOW-STOOLS,
HEIGHT AND PROJECTION OF STUCCO CORNICES,
AND INTERIOR FINISH, WITH MANY
VALUABLE TABLES.

By A. J. BRYAN, Architect.

SAN FRANCISCO:
A. L. BANCROFT & CO., PRINTERS AND LITHOGRAPHERS,
721 Market Street,
1880.

PREFACE.

VERY few general rules in architectural proportion can be applied to every style of architecture. Special cases can only be provided for by the ingenuity of the Architect. Our aim has been to avoid extremes, and furnish only such practical rules as, in our judgment, seem best adapted to the requirements of all classes of buildings in this country. While the rules and plates are our own, it is but just to say that we have freely consulted the works of many authors on the subject, and have carefully compared the practical results from other and more complicated rules with the results obtained by the application of the simple and comprehensive ones contained herein, which, added to our own experience, enables us to offer this volume to the Building Fraternity with the assurance that the measures given are in accord with the works of the best masters. The tables are introduced in the belief that they will obviate the necessity of many calculations, acquaint the novice with the relative proportions of the members of a column, and serve as a ready reference for all persons who are interested in building.

A. J. BRYAN.

CHICO, CALIFORNIA, 1880.

CONTENTS.

PLATE I.

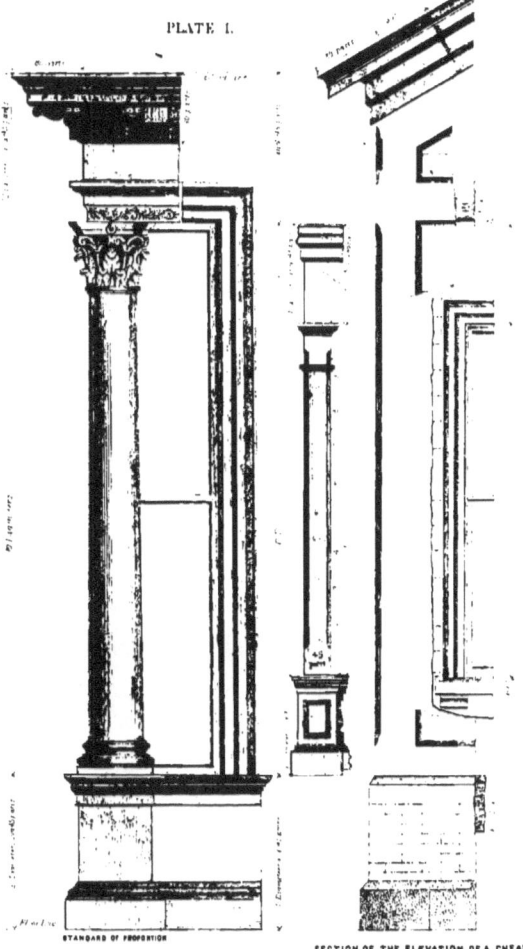

INTERIOR ELEVATION OF A WINDOW AND ROOM BASE.

SECTION OF THE ELEVATION OF A CHEAP
ONE STORY DWELLING WITH PLAIN
RAKING CORNICE.

ARCHITECTURAL PROPORTION.

THAT the ancient Orders of Architecture have received their full share of attention from writers in all ages no one can doubt. Many excellent works contain elaborate descriptions of the beautiful proportions of the *Five Orders*, and merited criticisms on the present styles, while very few contain any practical system which can be used for the improvement of the interior and exterior appearance of the thousands of buildings which are being erected each year in this country.

Architecture, like any other invention of man, is susceptible of improvement. The finished building is only the reflex of the designer's knowledge of the fitness of things. A justly proportioned building is pleasing to the eye, while it has no part that will attract particular attention—a finely formed body, with ornaments of natural form and members of just magnitude.

Architectural proportion is the relation one part or member of a building bears to others, and can exist only in the combination of a number of things of unequal size. A square building has no proportion between length, width and height, and at best is a poor example of architecture.

The student cannot devote too much time to the study of the best examples of classical architecture, yet, after all his study and research, when he is called upon to design dwellings and other buildings which are suited to the requirements of modern civilization, he may be able to talk learnedly about architecture as an art, and still have no idea how his knowledge of ancient architecture will enable him to give just proportions to the members of an ordinary building.

High art is a popular text for much writing, but unfortunately those who discourse most upon that worthy theme seem to practice it with the least degree of intelligence in their designs. Unnatural forms in ornamentation and uniform widths for the members of stories of different heights, which are so often found in the designs of impracticable theorists, are, of themselves, a bar to pleasant variety in a design, and the essence of bad taste in architecture.

As the proportions of classic architecture are not applicable to modern buildings, or to cheap buildings of any style, new ratios must be introduced, so as to modify the ancient Orders, or produce new ones. The *Five Orders* of *Architecture*, known as the *Doric*, *Ionic*, *Corinthian*, *Tuscan* and *Composite*, were each suited to a particular purpose and style of building.

After the return of the Heracleidæ, the Dorians, who afterwards founded Sparta, Argos and Messenia, introduced the *Doric Order* into the Peloponesus, about 1104 B. C. That they were the first inventors of that Order is very probable, because the massive proportions of the earliest examples were particularly suited to the *purposes* of architecture in the Peloponesus during the reign of the Hellenic tribes.

The Ionic colonies of Asia Minor gratified their taste and supplied their wants, in an architectural sense, by introducing the Order which bears their name. The Greek Architects, Callicrates, Ictinus, Pericles and Phidias, built the celebrated Parthenon at Athens, in the Doric Order, about 440 B. C., and Callierates is credited with inventing the *Corinthian Order*, which was not in general use in Greece before the time of Alexander the Great; the oldest example in Greece being the Choragic Monument of Lysicrates, built 335 B. C.

The *Tuscan Order* is of doubtful origin, and was probably never extensively used, while the Triumphal Arches erected by the Romans to commemorate great victories, brought into use the excessively ornamented column known as the *Composite Order*.

If we go further back into the history of architecture and take account of *Assyrian Architecture* on the plains of Mesopotamia; *Egyptian Architecture* as applied to the temples of the Theban kings, of whom, Osirtesen reigned 1640 B. C., we are led to believe that architecture was reduced to something like a science long before even the *Doric Order* was invented.

In ancient architecture, the column was the prominent feature, and in many excellent examples, the column constituted the whole Order. First among the distinguishing features was the ratio of the height of the shaft to its diameter, or *vice versa*. To find the height of the shaft, or the size of any member, it was first necessary to know the diameter, hence the practice of making the diameter of the shaft the basis of all calculations in architecture. And it seems that so long as this practice was strictly followed, architecture improved, natural and beautiful forms were blended, so as to produce capitals and ornaments in some of the Orders that challenge the admiration of all men, while the proportions of some examples of the ancient Orders approximate perfection. The perfection to which the ancient Orders attained was not due to the efforts or inventions of any one man, but to the combined efforts of men of different generations, each striving to carry the Order to a higher degree of perfection.

PLATE 11.

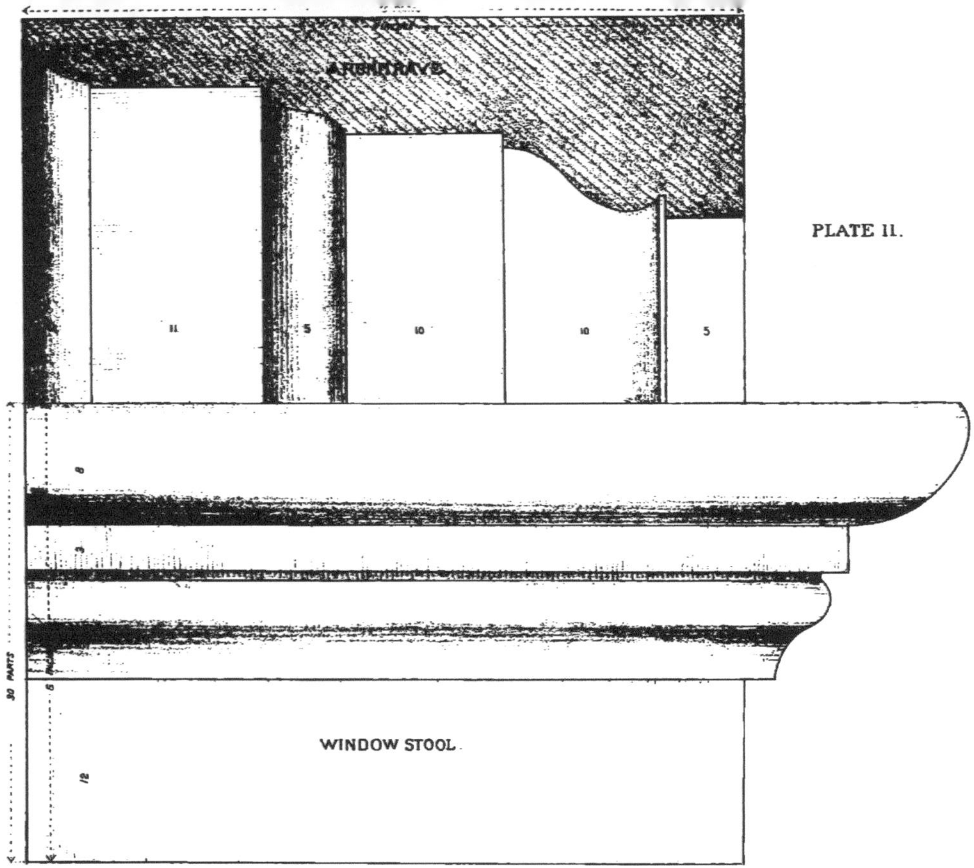
ARCHITRAVE
11
5
10
10
5
8
3
6
12
30 PARTS
WINDOW STOOL.

Full credence must not be given to stories claiming that the best specimens of the old Orders were the first given, since this is not the truth. Nor do we give more credence to what is related concerning the accomplishments of the ancient architects, for it seems unreasonable to say that an architect could learn more of each art and science, than a man who gave his whole time to the study of any one in particular, yet we know some of the ancient architects wrote on all the sciences. Pythius, Architect of the Temple of Minerva, at Priene, says: "An architect should have that perfect knowledge of each art and science, which is not even acquired by the professors in any one in particular, who have had every opportunity of improving themselves in it." It should be the pride of every honest and unselfish architect to so construct his buildings that others who follow the profession after his time, may copy or improve upon his inventions.

Architects who expect to succeed in their profession must work from a principle when working out their designs. Buildings designed so that the size of each member is governed by the number of minutes contained in the corresponding member on the standard of proportion used, will always be worth something as a work of art, for they are the embodiment of a principle which is manifest in every detail, and like an imperfect machine, the standard may be improved until it approximates perfection. Should an architect wish to introduce new ratios between the members of his work, he must first apply them to an Order, or a Standard of Proportion, then if they are found to produce well balanced and suitable members for a column, and are applicable to the interior and exterior finish of a building designed to fulfill the present *purposes* of architecture, his system will be completed. But to give heights to the members of the finish for the interior of the building, which could not with propriety be given to the members of a column equal in height to the clear height of the room or story, is wrong, because the purposes of architecture at the present time require an equality of ratios between the members of the interior and exterior work.

A standard of proportion is as essential to a building of any kind, as it is to know the diameter of the shaft before computing the size of the members of a column. Architects who use their eye for their standard of proportion are never able to defend their work in a contest, for they have no principle or system in their designs.

Many writers attempt to convey the idea that all examples of any of the *Five Orders* were alike, but such teachings are not founded upon truth. It is right and proper for

any man to select what *he* thinks is the best example of any given Order, and praise it as much as he chooses, but it is not right for him to give his example to the public as *the* Order, when he knows that nearly all other examples of the Order differ from the one which he has selected.

We are willing to accord to the architects of ancient times the very highest degree of intelligence, but are not prepared to believe one-half of the *bosh* that has been written about every crooked wall, deformed arch, or other imperfection found in any ancient temple, being put in for effect, and due to the superior intelligence of the architect, for if it is, or ever was, necessary to deform an object or body in order to make it look well, few sensible men will follow the example.

As the temples of the ancients cannot be copied for present use, we shall now direct our attention to a standard of proportion which is intended to apply to a cheaper class of buildings, better suited to the wants of the American people, and the purposes of architecture in this country.

To clearly show the necessity for a standard of proportion we have introduced the column shown in *Plate I.* As a standard of proportion it is applicable to all classes of buildings. The diameter of the shaft above the base is divided into 60 minutes or units of measure. The taper of the shaft is one-sixth of one diameter, or 50 minutes in diameter at the neck below the fillet and astragal. The height of the principal members are: Pedestal base, 50 minutes; die, 85 minutes; cornice, 50 minutes; shaft base, 30 minutes; shaft, including base and capital, 10 diameters; capital, above the fillet and astragal, 1 diameter and 10 minutes; architrave, 45 minutes; frieze, 40 minutes; cornice, 80 minutes—whole height of the column or Order, $15\frac{1}{2}$ diameters. Referring to *Plate I* it will be seen that the three major divisions of the column are so arranged that, for vertical proportion, they, are applicable to the three major divisions of the elevation of an interior wall, and *vice versa.* *First:* The height of the pedestal is equal to the distance from the floor line to the top of the window-stool; *Second:* The whole height of the shaft equals the height of the perpendicular architrave for the window, or the distance from the top of the window-stool to the soffit or lowest edge of the horizontal architrave; *Third:* The height of the entablature is equal to the distance from the soffit to the ceiling line.

Of the minor divisions of the column, the pedestal base gives the proper height for the room base, the height of the window-stool or sill equals the height of the pedestal cornice, and the height of the architrave or lowest division of the entablature governs the width of the window architrave.

Each member or part of the interior finish contains the same number of minutes or units

PLATE III.

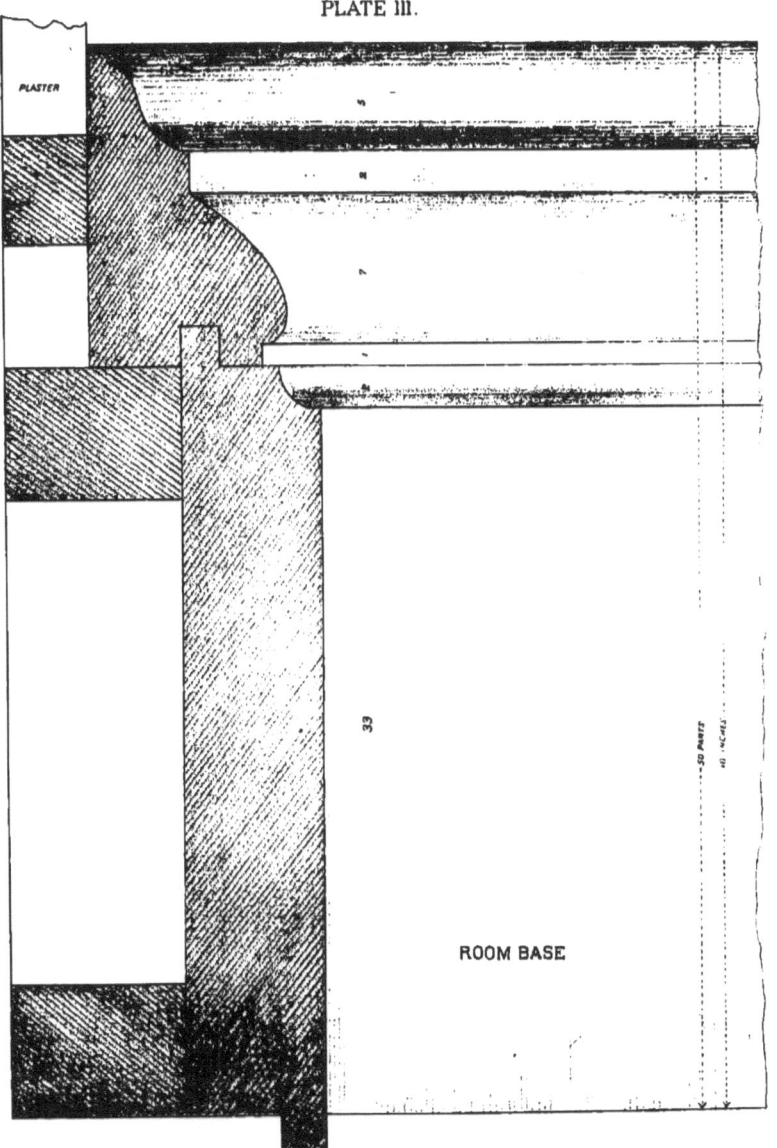

PLASTER

ROOM BASE

of measure as is given to the corresponding member on the column. This system of proportion gives perfect harmony between the interior and exterior finish, is easily understood and applied, and has but one basis from which the size of any part or member of the building is computed. No amount of decoration can hide the vulgar appearance of a room if the window openings show a greater or less height than the corresponding part of the column from which the height of all members of the interior finish is computed. The room base, die and window-stool of any room represent the three divisions of the pedestal of a column as clearly on the elevation of the interior wall as the same members do on a pedestal surmounted by a shaft and entablature. The height of the window architrave must represent the height of the shaft of the Order, because it rests upon the pedestal and supports the horizontal architrave or lowest division of the entablature. To complete the Order on the interior wall elevation, the stucco cornice must contain as many minutes in height and projection as given to the height and projection of the cornice or upper division of the entablature on the standard of proportion.

We dismiss, for the present, Architectural Proportion, and take up a subject equally important and often criminally neglected:

FOUNDATIONS.

A good foundation is the key to success in everything, and without it a fine house is only a costly sham. When the walls and plaster of a new building begin to crack. it is usually charged to climatic influences, yet, in nearly every case, the cause can be traced directly to a faulty foundation. Good walls, with broad footings of stone or hard-burned brick. will always give the owner of a building better satisfaction than he can receive from a hundred theories that work well only on paper.

To insure a good foundation all walls should start from a common level, either at the bottom of the basement, or, if no basement is required, then in trenches excavated to a sufficient depth to insure equal resistance from the ground. A good foundation at one place is often an insufficient one for the same building even on an adjoining lot. Therefore, it is always advisable for the architect to visit the building site *after* the excavating is done, when he will readily detect any great inequality in the density of the earth along the line of the walls, and will then be competent to make a suitable foundation for that particular place. The width of foundation and basement walls should always be liberal and rather more than appears, after examination of the under-

lying earth, to be necessary. If extravagance can be justified at all in the erection of a building, the foundation should have the lion's share; and he who cannot afford to build upon a good foundation will soon regret having built at all, for upon the solidity of the foundation depends the lasting beauty, usefulness, and safety of the whole superstructure.

As the safety of the whole superstructure depends upon the *solidity*, so also does the exterior appearance of an isolated building depend, in a large degree, upon the *height* of the foundation.

A two or three story dwelling with the first-floor line only one and a half or two feet above the level of the ground, presents the appearance of having settled after completion; and a low building with a very high foundation has the appearance of having been raised above high water mark. In either case the architect who designs such buildings usually makes them bear false witness against the locality wherein they are erected.

As an illustration of Rule I, we will refer the reader to the section of the elevation of a cottage and foundation shown in *Plate I.* The clear height of the story in the cottage is 10 feet, or equal to the height of the column shaft shown in the same *Plate*, and as the diameter of the shaft is the basis from which the height and projection of the members of the column is computed, we take the height of the story as the representative of the shaft; and divide this height into 10 diameters and then divide one diameter into 60 parts for the unit of measure which, in this case, equals ⅗ or ! of an inch. Proceeding then as with a column, the height of the foundation to the floor line is made to equal 2 diameters and 45 minutes, or 2 feet 9 inches. The height of the stone base to the foundation is made to equal 50 minutes or 10 inches, and the height of the water-table equals 30 minutes or 6 inches.

Then beginning at the ceiling line 2 diameters and 45 minutes, or 2 feet 9 inches is laid up for the height of the entablature, or the distance from the ceiling line to the eaves.

As the cornice on the standard is 80 minutes in height and projection, the height of the cottage cornice measured at right angles from the slant of the roof, and the inclined and end projection is made to equal 80 minutes, or 1 foot 4 inches.

The members of the cornice on the dwelling contain the same number of minutes, or units of measure, as is given to the corresponding member of the cornice on the standard, with this exception: one member is left out of the corona in the cottage cornice, and its height is added to the height of the bed mould in order to give that

PLATE IV.

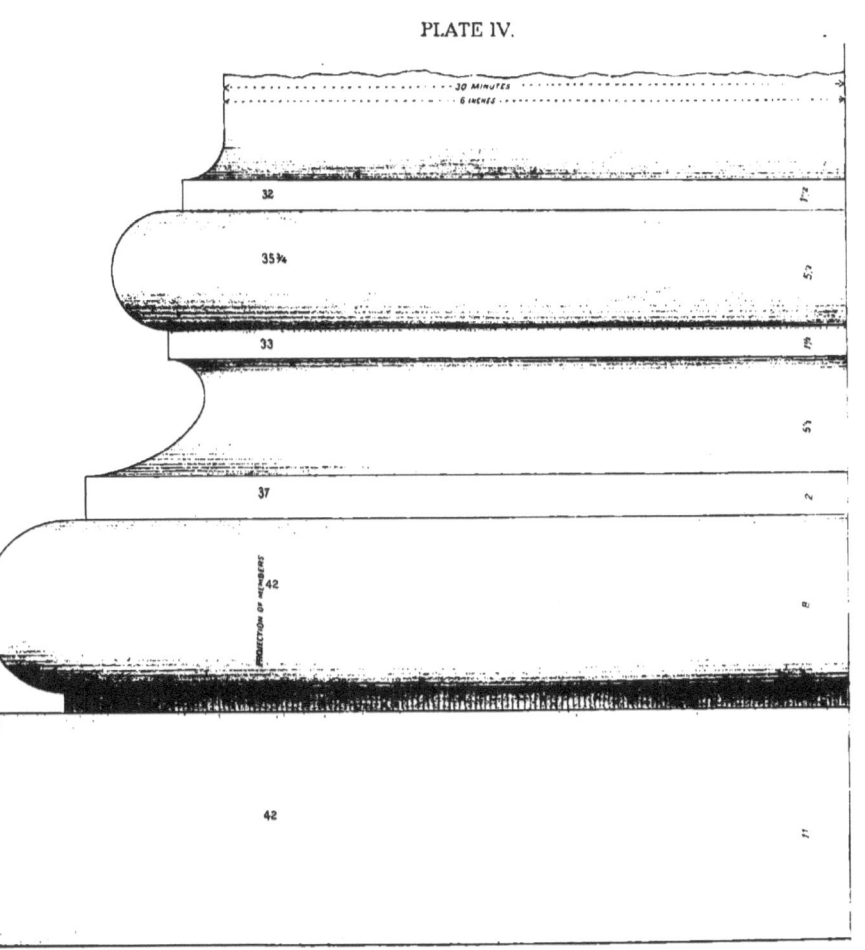

BASE of SHAFT.

member more prominence in its retired position in the raking cornice, and the height of the dental course and spiral mould next below are both given to the lowest division of the plain cornice.

Plate I also represents the standard of proportion as standing in a room, the clear height of which equals 15 feet 6 inches. Then in order to keep the same ratios between the members of the interior story finish of the cottage and the members of the column, it becomes necessary to reduce the standard of proportion, until it will stand in a room or story which is only 10 feet in height. This we do by reducing 10 feet to hundredths or thousandths of inches and dividing by 15½. The quotient resulting therefrom will be the diameter of the shaft of the reduced column.

The sum obtained for the diameter is then subdivided into 60 minutes, and one minute, or the unit of measure thus found for the 10-foot story, is increased as many times for the height of each member of the story finish as there are minutes in the height of the corresponding member on the standard example. 120.000 inches ÷ 15½ = 7.₁₀⁵₀ inches for the diameter of the shaft of the reduced column. 7.740 ÷ 60 = .₁₂₉₀ inches for the unit of measure for the 10-foot story. .129×50 = 6.₄₅⁵₀ inches for the height of the room base for the cottage. .129×30 = 3.₅₆⁵₀ inches for the height of the window-stool and sill. 7.74 ÷ 10 = 77.₄⁵₀ inches, or 6 feet 5.₄⁵₀ inches for the height of the window architrave, or the distance from the top of the window-stool to the soffit above the window. .129×45 = 5.₆₅⁵₀ inches for the width of the window architraves. .129×80 = 10.₃₂⁵₀ inches for the height and projection of the stucco cornice in the cottage or any story which has a height of just 10 feet.

It will be seen that the members on the interior elevation of the room contain exactly as many parts or minutes in height as is given to the corresponding members on the standard, and that there is a perfect equality of ratios between the members of the exterior and interior work.

In *Plate I* is also shown the elevation of the veranda post, balustrade, and part elevation of the cornice. As the whole height from the floor line to the top of the cornice is 10 feet, the denomination of the unit of measure for the verandah finish is .₁₂₉₀ inches, or the same as for the interior story. Commencing at the floor line of the verandah, the plinth, or plain part of the pedestal base is 33 minutes in height, as on the standard, and the moulded part 17 minutes in height, making the whole height of the base equal 50 minutes. .129×33 = 4.₂₅⁵₀ inches. .129×17 = 2.₁₉⁵₀ inches. .129×85 = 10.₉₆⁵₀ inches for the height of the pedestal die. .129×30 = 3.₅₆⁵₀ inches for the height of the pedestal cornice. 7.74×10 = 6 feet 5.₄⁵₀ inches for the height of the

PLATE V.

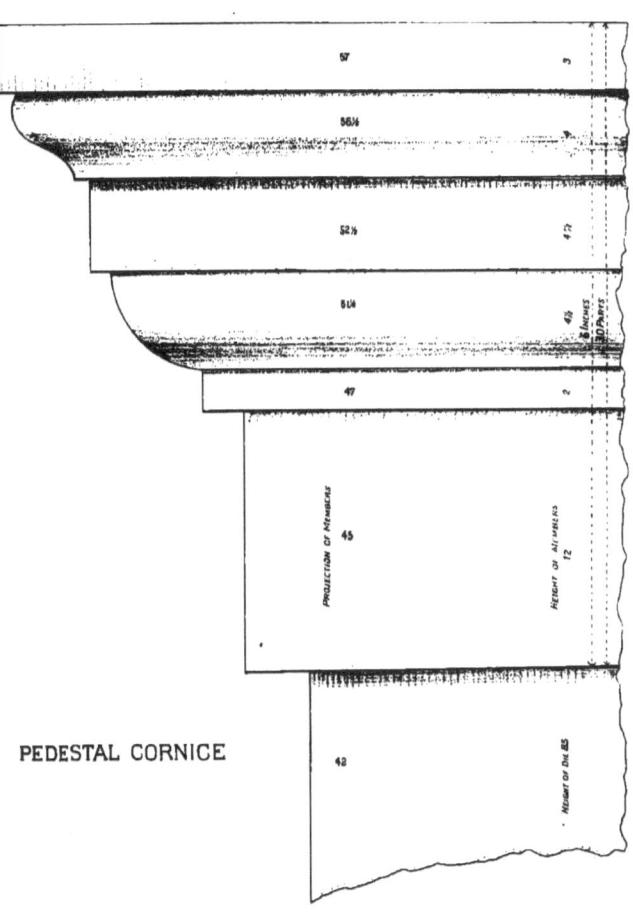

PEDESTAL CORNICE

post above the pedestal. .129×45= 5$\frac{33}{100}$ inches for the diameter of the post. Eighty-five minutes—the height of the architrave and frieze on the standard—multiplied by .129 10.965 inches for the height of the bracket, spandrel, or other finish, between the top of the post and the lowest line of the cornice. .129×80 10$\frac{32}{100}$ inches for the height and projection of the verandah cornice.

Inasmuch as the diameter of the post equals $\frac{7}{8}$ of the diameter of a round shaft of the same length, to find the projection of the die and other members from the center of the post, the unit of measure is multiplied by $\frac{7}{8}$ of the number of parts given for the projection of the members of the pedestal of the standard.

Plate II shows a section of the window-stool and architrave for the window shown in *Plate I*, for a story 15 feet 6 inches clear. The length of the architrave or casing is 10 feet and its width 9 inches, or 45 parts of one diameter. The principal members of the side architraves for the openings contain the same number of parts as is given to the members of the entablature architrave shown in *Plate IX*. Two members are added to the lowest part, or inner edge of the architraves for the windows and doors, in order to break up the plain surface of that part of the architrave which is covered by a wreath in the entablature.

Plate III shows a section of the room base with the height of each member given. The drawings are merely intended to illustrate the rules and show the number of parts that are given to each member. The *form* of the members for the story finish can be varied to suit the fancy of the designer.

Plate IV shows the shaft base and the height and projection of each member from the center of the shaft.

Plate V shows the height and projection of the members of the pedestal cornice and the projection of the die from the central line. The height and projection of the members of the capital are shown in *Plate VI*, and require no explanation.

The cornice or upper division of the entablature, is shown on a large scale in *Plate VII*. The modillions may be carved and ornamented, or left plain, as the style of the work requires.

From the entablatures of street fronts, which are elevated above the standard of proportion, it is not necessary to exclude any of the minor members, for the denomination of the unit of measure will be increased as the entablature is elevated, consequently the size of each member will be increased in its proper ratio; but from entablatures for any part of a building where the denomination of the unit of measure is decreased, as the elevation is increased above the first floor line, the minor members should be excluded, and the principal ones enlarged.

PLATE VI.

CAPITAL

A facade with portico, and window and door entablatures in any Order, and having a simple cornice at the greatest elevation, is the reverse of good taste, or any rule in architecture; but entablatures for the building and portico may be used with good effect, when there are no entablatures, or even projecting architraves on the window and door openings.

It is hardly proper to support a portico entablature with square posts, or to place a cornice without frieze or architrave, above the round shafts of any Order; but pilasters projected one-half the width of their face from the wall, and having capitals, may be properly set under the entablatures of street fronts or other facades.

The proper divisions of a simple cornice are represented in *Plate VIII*, also the projection of the members from the face of the wall. In all *Plates* showing parts of the finish or members of the column, the figures give the projection of the members from the center of the shaft, or what is usually called the axis of the column.

The principal members of the cornices shown in *Plates VII and VIII*, contain the same number of minutes in height; and the projection of the square of the cymatium in *Plate VII* from the face of the frieze, is equal to the projection of the corresponding member in *Plate VIII* from the wall line, which would be the face of the frieze in an entablature.

Plate IX represents a large scale drawing of the architrave, or lowest division of the entablature of the standard of proportion shown in *Plate I*. The form of the lowest member is well adapted to the proper shading of vine or wreath ornaments, projected sufficiently from the retired face of the member to give the leaves a natural and varied appearance, but for ordinary work this member may be left without ornamentation.

Plate X with the explanations, fully illustrates our system of reducing superimposed stories. We are aware that this is a grave departure from the rules and usages of many architects, and that it does not at all conform to the *Alisona Photago* example, if the eminent art critic who made use of that illustration intended it to apply to superimposed stories, for the system which *Plate X* illustrates, does not reduce the superimposed stories so much, and particularly the *third* and *fourth* ones shown in the section.

Examples of lateral or vertical proportion taken from old palaces or churches, built hundreds of years ago, may be interesting as a study, but they have no practical value in the architecture of this country.

From an author and architect of the present day, we have an example now before us in which each superimposed story is just *two feet less* in height than the one next below. This system reduces the superimposed stories so *fast* that the fourth-story windows appear to be almost square.

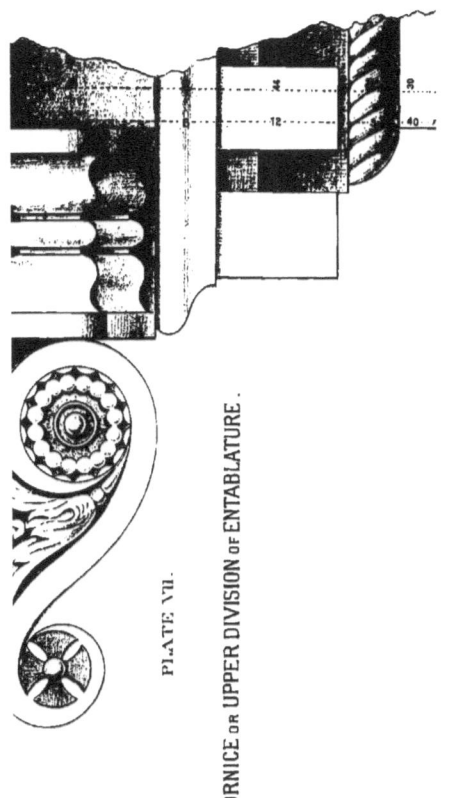

PLATE VII.

CORNICE OR UPPER DIVISION OF ENTABLATURE.

It must be remembered that feet and inches are not the units of measure in architecture, and that all heights and widths should first be found in diameters and minutes, and the height of superimposed stories by the multiplication or division of the unit of measure used for the first story. After a measure has been determined in the proper way, it may be reduced to feet or inches, and used as such, but not before, without confusion.

The system which we here introduce for finding the height of superimposed stories is to make the unit of measure used for the *second* story equal seven-eighths of the unit used for the *first* story; and the unit for the *third* story to equal seven-eighths of the unit of the *second;* the unit for the *fourth* story seven-eighths of the unit of the *third;* and so on through all of the stories. Then the proportion is: As the height of the *first* is to the height of the *second,* so is the height of the *third* to the height of the *fourth.* Each horizontal space of *dead* wall between the openings is diminished in the same ratio; also the height of each superimposed opening and the finish thereof, and the height of all interior story finish.

In *Plate X* an outline sketch of the standard of proportion is shown in each story. As the first story is 15 feet 6 inches clear—the whole height of the standard of proportion—the diameter for that story is one foot, and the unit of measure is .62 inches. We will give one series of explanations, and show the application of the rules to each story and the finish thereof. (See Rules VI, VII, VIII.) For the base of the first story, we multiply the unit of the measure by the number of minutes contained in the height of the pedestal base of the standard of proportion (see Rule IX). .20·50·50 inches for the height of the room base, including the mould. Rule X—.20·33·6½ inches for the base plinth, leaving 3½½ inches for the height of the moulded part. Rule XI—.20×30·6 inches for the height of the window-stool and sill. Rule XII—.42·10·120 inches, or 10 feet, for the height of the interior window architrave, or the distance from the top of the window-stool to the soffit above the window. Rule XIII—.20·45·9 inches, for the width of the window architrave. Rule XIV—.20·80·16 inches, for the height and projection of the stucco cornice in the first story. Rule XV gives .54¼ inches for the unit of measure for the second story. Rule XVI—.175·60·10⅝ inches for the diameter. Rule XVII—10.50×15¼·13 feet 6⅝ inches for the clear height of the second story. Again applying the rules for finding the height and width of the story finish, we get 8⅞½ inches for the height of the room-base in the second story, for the window-stool and sill, 5⅞½ inches, window architrave, 8 feet 9 inches in height, and 7⅞½ inches in width, and 1 foot 2 inches for the height and projection of the stucco cornice. After reducing ⅞½ inches in accordance with Rule XV, we get ⅞½ inches for

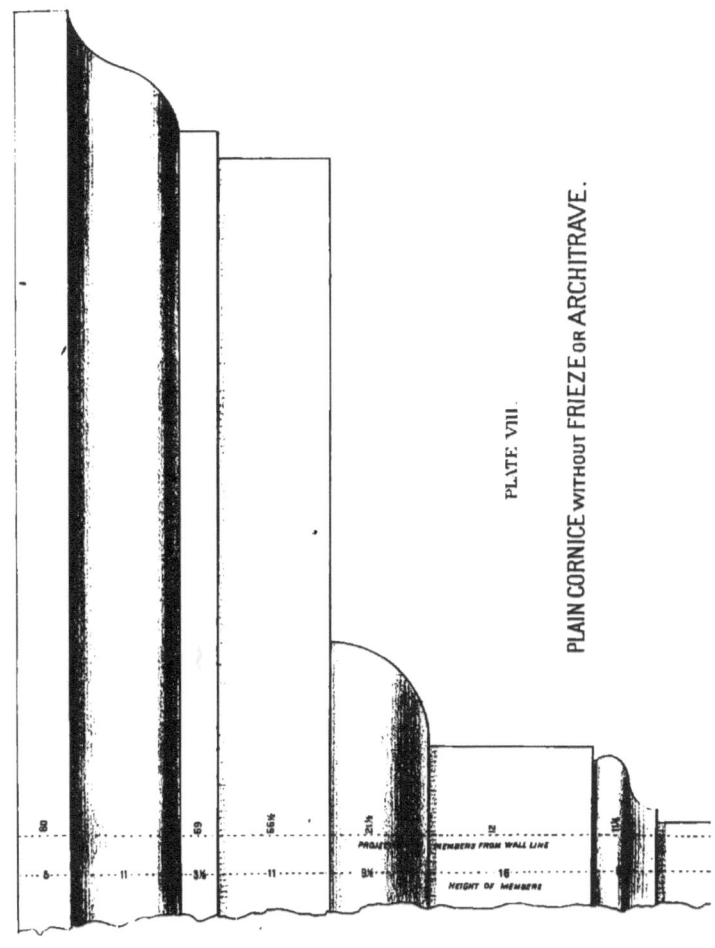

PLATE: VIII.

PLAIN CORNICE without FRIEZE or ARCHITRAVE.

the unit of measure, 9ᵢₒₒ inches for the diameter, and 11 feet 10ᵢₒₒ inches for the clear height of the third story. Applying the rules as before, the height of the room base is 7ᵢₒₒ inches, window-stool and sill, 4ᵢₒₒ inches, window architrave, 7 feet 7ᵢₒₒ inches in height, and 6ᵢₒₒ inches in width, and the height and projection of the stucco cornice for the third story 12ᵢₒₒ inches. For the fourth story the unit is ᵢₒₒ inches, diameter 8ᵢₒₒ inches, and the clear height 10 feet 4ᵢₒₒ inches. Height of base, 6ᵢₒₒ inches, window-stool and sill, 4ᵢₒₒ inches, length or height of window architrave, 6 feet 8ᵢₒₒ inches, and width 6ᵢₒₒ inches, height and projection of the stucco cornice in the fourth story, 10ᵢₒₒ inches.

The depth of the beams including floor and plaster, is equal to 80 units of the story below them, but their depth will, of course, always depend upon the width of the span, and the safe load they are intended to carry. The interior elevation of each story presents the outline of a complete Order, as shown in the following comparative table:

	COLUMN.		PARTS		STORY.		PARTS
Height of Pedestal Base			50	Height of Room Base			50
"	"	" Die	85	"		Die	85
"	"	" Cornice	30	"		" Window-Stool.	30
"	" Shaft, 10 dia.			"		Window Casing. 10 dia.	
"	" Architrave,		45	"		Window Architrave,	45
"	" Frieze		40	"		Frieze	40
"	" Cornice		80	"		Stucco Cornice	80
	Whole height, 15½ dia.				Whole height, 15½ dia.		

Many devices have been resorted to by authors for finding the height of entablatures or cornices which are elevated above their standard of proportion, but all are more or less complicated; and a great many of them amount to nothing more than an intelligent guess. The system which we will now introduce is very simple and probably has as many claims to excellence as the best that are in use.

The lowest line of the entablature on the standard of proportion which we have introduced for this work is 12 feet 9 inches above the floor line. Up to that elevation the height of portico or wall entablatures is found by dividing the distance they are elevated above the floor line by 12¾—the number of diameters contained in the combined height of the pedestal and shaft; and then by multiplying the quotient by 2¾—the number of diameters contained in the height of the entablature.

By referring to the tables where ᵢₒₒ inches is the unit of measure, it will be seen

PLATE IX.

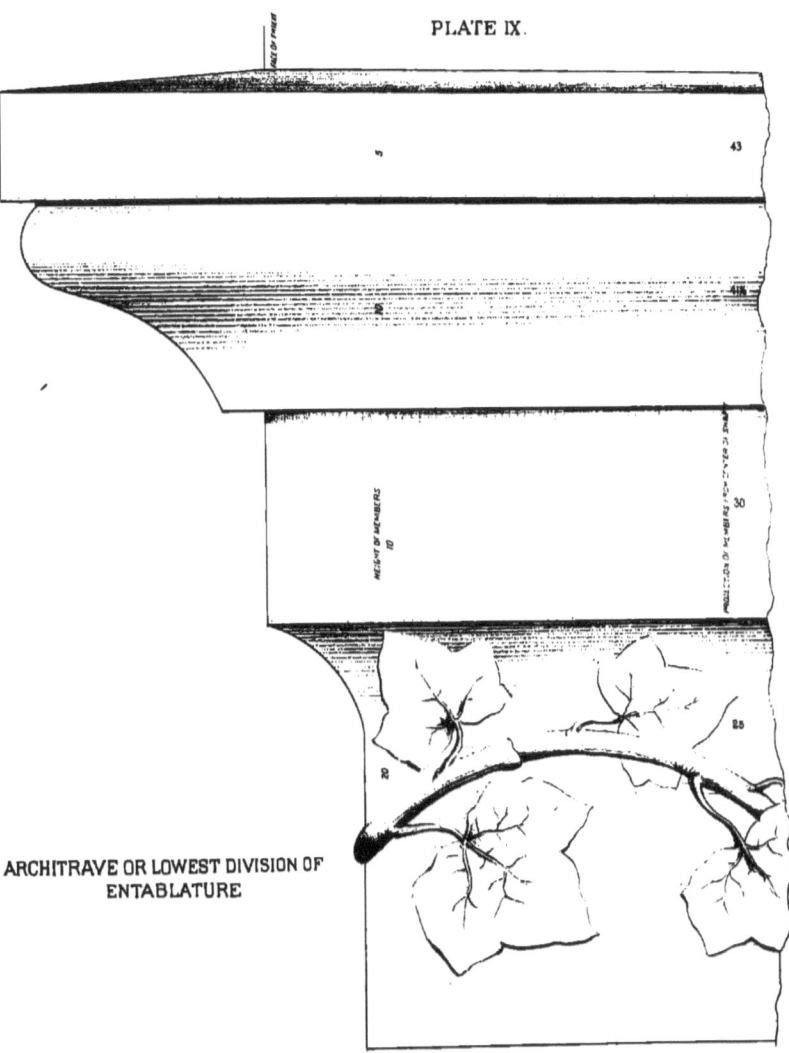

43

30

25

20

ARCHITRAVE OR LOWEST DIVISION OF
ENTABLATURE

that the distance from the floor line to the entablature is 12 feet $1\frac{00}{100}$ inches, or $7\frac{00}{100}$ inches less than the height just given from the standard of proportion. Then, as the addition of $\frac{1}{100}$ inches to the unit of measure increases the combined height of the pedestal and shaft, $7\frac{00}{100}$ inches, it seems that the most reasonable way to reduce entablatures below what an Order would make them, if continued to an indefinite height, would be to increase the distance between the minutes, that is, make the distance between $1\frac{00}{100}$ inches and $1\frac{1}{100}$ inches a little more than $7\frac{00}{100}$ inches—the distance between $1\frac{00}{100}$ inches and $1\frac{00}{100}$ inches; and continue that increase in regular ratios indefinitely.

The following table gives the proper elevation at which the different units from $\frac{00}{100}$ inches to $1\frac{00}{100}$ inches are used; also the height of the entablature at each point or elevation, and the projection from the face of the frieze. This table was calculated in the manner above explained, and we leave it to others in practice to make the distance between the points where the different units are used greater or less, as the style of their work requires.

PLATE X.

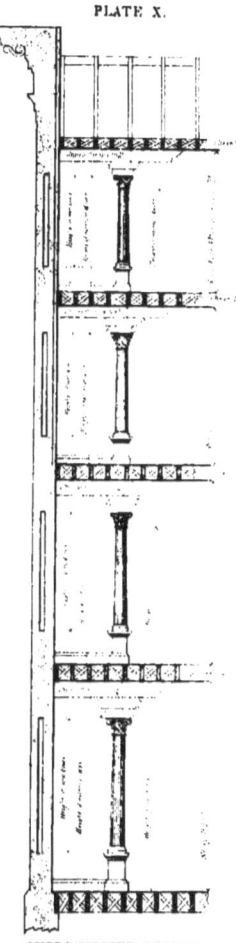

SUPERIMPOSED STORIES.

TABLE SHOWING THE HEIGHT AND PROJECTION OF ENTABLATURES WHICH ARE ELEVATED ABOVE THE STANDARD OF PROPORTION.

Elevation above Floor Line.	Unit of Measure.	Height of Entablature.	Projection from Face of Frieze.	Elevation above Floor Line.	Unit of Measure.	Height of Entablature.	Projection from Face of Frieze.
13:4.70	.21	2:10.65	1:4.80	27:7.50	.37	5:1.05	2:5.60
14:0.50	.22	3:0.30	1:5.60	28:11.70	.38	5:2.70	2:6.40
14:8.45	.23	3:1.95	1:6.40	30:4.85	.39	5:4.35	2:7.20
15:4.60	.24	3:3.60	1:7.20	31:11.00	.40	5:6.00	2:8.00
16:1.00	.25	3:5.25	1:8.00	33:6.20	.41	5:7.65	2:8.80
16:9.70	.26	3:6.90	1:8.80	35:2.50	.42	5:9.30	2:9.60
17:6.75	.27	3:8.55	1:9.60	36:11.95	.43	5:10.95	2:10.40
18:4.20	.28	3:10.20	1:10.40	38:10.60	.44	6:0.60	2:11.20
19:2.10	.29	3:11.85	1:11.20	40:10.50	.45	6:2.25	3:0.00
20:0.50	.30	4:1.50	2:0.00	42:11.70	.46	6:3.90	3:0.80
20:11.45	.31	4:3.15	2:0.80	45:2.25	.47	6:5.55	3:1.60
21:11.00	.32	4:4.80	2:1.60	47:6.20	.48	6:7.20	3:2.40
22:11.20	.33	4:6.45	2:2.40	49:11.60	.49	6:8.85	3:3.20
24:0.10	.34	4:8.10	2:3.20	52:6.50	.50	6:10.50	3:4.00
25:1.75	.35	4:9.75	2:4.00	55:2.95	.51	7:0.15	3:4.80
26:4.20	.36	4:11.40	2:4.80	58:1.00	.52	7:1.80	3:5.60

RULES.

Rule I.—To find the height of foundation for a one-story isolated building: divide the clear height of the story into 10 diameters, and make the height of the foundation to the floor line equal $2\frac{3}{4}$ diameters.

Rule II.—To find the distance from the ceiling line of a one-story building to the lowest line of the eaves: divide the clear height of the story into 10 diameters, and make the distance from the ceiling line to the eaves equal $2\frac{3}{4}$ diameters.

Rule III.—To find the height and projection of the cornice for a one-story building: divide the clear height of the story into 10 diameters, and make the height and projection of the cornice equal $1\frac{1}{3}$ diameters, or 80 minutes.

Rule IV.—To find the height of the stone base for a foundation: divide one diameter into 60 minutes, and make the height of the base equal 50 minutes.

Rule V.—To find the height of the water-table: divide one diameter into 60 minutes, and make the height of the water-table equal 30 minutes.

Rule VI.—To find the diameter of the shaft when the whole height of the column (pedestal, shaft and entablature) is given: divide the height by $15\frac{1}{2}$.

Rule VII.—To find the proper diameter of any story: divide the clear height of the story by $15\frac{1}{2}$.

Rule VIII.—To find the unit of measure for any story: divide the diameter by 60.

Rule IX.—To find the whole height of the room-base for any story: multiply the unit of measure by 50.

Rule X.—To find the height of the plinth, or plain part of the room-base: multiply the unit of measure by 33.

Rule XI.—To find the height of the window-stool, or sill, for any story: multiply the unit of measure by 30.

Rule XII.—To find the height of the interior window casing or architrave for any story: multiply the diameter of the story by 10.

Rule XIII.—To find the width of the window-architrave for any story: multiply the unit of measure by 45.

Rule XIV.—To find the height and projection of the stucco cornice for any story: multiply the unit of measure by 80.

Rule XV.—To find the unit of measure for any superimposed story: take $\frac{7}{8}$ of the unit used for the story next below.

Rule XVI.—To find the diameter of any superimposed story: multiply the unit of measure by 60.

Rule XVII.—To find the clear height of any superimposed story: multiply the diameter by $15\frac{1}{2}$.

Rule XVIII.—To find the width of any door or window architrave, or the diameter of a post: divide the height into 10 diameters and make the width equal 45 minutes, or $\frac{3}{4}$ of one diameter.

Rule XIX.—To find the width of a pilaster: divide the height into 10 diameters, and make the width equal 50 minutes, or $\frac{5}{6}$ of one diameter.

Rule XX.—To find the width of any single door or window: divide the height into 10 diameters, and make the width equal $4\frac{1}{2}$ diameters.

TABLE OF COLUMN FINISH.

Length of Shaft.	Diameter of Shaft above Base.	Diameter of Shaft at Neck.	Height of Capital.	Height of Shaft Base.	Whole height of Pedestal.	Height of Pedestal Base.	Height of Pedestal Cornice.	Distance from Floor Line to lowest Line of Entablature.	Height of Entablature.	Whole height of Column.	One Minute.
5:0.00	6.00	5.00	7.00	3.60	1:4.50	5.00	3.00	6:4.50	1:4.50	7:9.00	100
5:0.60	6.06	5.05	7.07	3.636	1:4.665	5.05	3.03	6:5.265	1:4.665	7:9.93	101
5:1.20	6.12	5.10	7.14	3.672	1:4.83	5.10	3.06	6:6.03	1:4.83	7:10.86	102
5:1.80	6.18	5.15	7.21	3.708	1:4.995	5.15	3.09	6:6.795	1:4.995	7:11.79	103
5:2.40	6.24	5.20	7.28	3.744	1:5.16	5.20	3.12	6:7.56	1:5.16	8:0.72	104
5:3.00	6.30	5.25	7.35	3.78	1:5.325	5.25	3.15	6:8.325	1:5.325	8:1.65	105
5:3.60	6.36	5.30	7.42	3.816	1:5.49	5.30	3.18	6:9.09	1:5.49	8:2.58	106
5:4.20	6.42	5.35	7.49	3.852	1:5.655	5.35	3.21	6:9.855	1:5.655	8:3.51	107
5:4.80	6.48	5.40	7.56	3.888	1:5.82	5.10	3.24	6:10.62	1:5.82	8:4.44	108
5:5.40	6.54	5.45	7.63	3.924	1:5.985	5.45	3.27	6:11.385	1:5.985	8:5.37	109
5:6.00	6.60	5.50	7.70	3.96	1:6.15	5.50	3.30	7:0.15	1:6.15	8:6.30	110
5:6.60	6.66	5.55	7.77	3.996	1:6.315	5.53	3.33	7:0.915	1:6.315	8:7.23	111
5:7.20	6.72	5.60	7.84	4.032	1:6.48	5.60	3.36	7:1.68	1:6.48	8:8.16	112
5:7.80	6.78	5.65	7.91	4.068	1:6.645	5.65	3.39	7:2.445	1:6.645	8:9.09	113
5:8.40	6.84	5.70	7.98	4.104	1:6.81	6.70	3.42	7:3.21	1:6.81	8:10.02	114
5:9.00	6.90	5.75	8.05	4.14	1:6.975	5.75	3.45	7:3.975	1:6.975	8:10.95	115
5:9.60	6.96	5.80	8.12	4.176	1:7.14	5.80	3.48	7:4.74	1:7.14	8:11.88	116
5:10.20	7.02	5.85	8.19	4.212	1:7.305	5.85	3.51	7:5.505	1:7.305	9:0.81	117
5:10.80	7.08	5.90	8.26	4.248	1:7.47	5.90	3.54	7:6.27	1:7.47	9:1.74	118
5:11.40	7.14	5.95	8.33	4.284	1:7.625	5.95	3.57	7:7.025	1:7.625	9:2.67	119
6:0.00	7.20	6.00	8.40	4.32	1:7.80	6.00	3.60	7:7.80	1:7.80	9:3.60	120
6:0.00	7.26	6.05	8.47	4.356	1:7.965	6.05	3.63	7:8.565	1:7.965	9:4.53	121
6:1.20	7.32	6.10	8.54	4.392	1:8.13	6.10	3.66	7:9.33	1:8.13	9:5.46	122
6:1.80	7.38	6.15	8.61	4.428	1:8.295	6.15	3.69	7:10.095	1:8.295	9:6.39	123
6:2.40	7.44	6.20	8.68	4.464	1:8.46	6.20	3.72	7:10.86	1:8.46	9:7.32	124

| Length of Interior Window Casing. | | | Distance from Floor Line to Top of Window Stool. | Height of Room Base or Skirting. | Height of Window Stool, or Sill. | Height of Exterior Doors. | Distance from Window Soffit to Ceiling. | Clear height of Story. | |

TABLE OF COLUMN FINISH.—*Continued.*

Length of Shaft.	Diameter of Shaft above Base.	Diameter of Shaft at Neck.	Height of Capital.	Height of Shaft Base.	Whole height of Pedestal.	Height of Pedestal Base.	Height of Pedestal Cornice.	Distance form Floor Line to Lower Line of Entablature.	Height of Entablature.	Whole height of Column.	One Minute.
6:3.00	7.50	6.25	8.75	4.50	1:8.625	6.25	3.75	7:11.625	1:8.625	9:8.25	.125
6:3.60	7.56	6.30	8.82	4.536	1:8.79	6.30	3.78	8:0.39	1:8.79	9:9.18	.126
6:4.20	7.62	6.35	8.89	4.576	1:8.955	6.35	3.81	8:1.155	1:8.955	9:10.11	.127
6:4.80	7.68	6.40	8.96	4.608	1:9.12	6.40	3.84	8:1.92	1:9.12	9:11.01	.128
6:5.40	7.74	6.45	9.03	4.644	1:9.285	6.45	3.87	8:2.685	1:9.285	9:11.97	.129
6:6.00	7.80	6.50	9.10	4.68	1:9.45	6.50	3.90	8:3.45	1:9.45	10:0.90	.130
6:6.60	7.86	6.55	9.17	4.716	1:9.615	6.55	3.93	8:4.215	1:9.615	10:1.83	.131
6:7.20	7.92	6.60	9.24	4.752	1:9.78	6.60	3.96	8:4.98	1:9.78	10:2.76	.132
6:7.80	7.98	6.65	9.31	4.788	1:9.915	6.65	3.99	8:5.745	1:9.915	10:3.69	.133
6:8.40	8.04	6.70	9.38	4.824	1:10.14	6.70	4.02	8:6.51	1:10.14	10:4.62	.134
6:9.00	8.10	6.75	9.45	4.86	1:10.275	6.75	4.05	8:7.275	1:10.275	10:5.55	.135
6:9.60	8.16	6.80	9.52	4.896	1:10.44	6.80	4.08	8:8.04	1:10.44	10:6.48	.136
6:10.20	8.22	6.85	9.59	4.932	1:10.605	6.85	4.11	8:8.805	1:10.605	10:7.41	.137
6:10.80	8.28	6.90	9.66	4.968	1:10.77	6.90	4.14	8:9.57	1:10.77	10:8.34	.138
6:11.40	8.34	6.95	9.73	5.004	1:10.935	6.95	4.17	8:10.335	1:10.935	10:9.27	.139
7:0.00	8.40	7.00	9.80	5.04	1:11.10	7.00	4.20	8:11.10	1:11.10	10:10.20	.140
7:0.60	8.46	7.05	9.87	5.076	1:11.265	7.05	4.23	8:11.865	1:11.265	10:11.13	.141
7:1.20	8.52	7.10	9.94	5.112	1:11.43	7.10	4.26	9:0.63	1:11.43	11:0.06	.142
7:1.80	8.58	7.15	10.01	5.148	1:11.595	7.15	4.29	9:1.395	1:11.595	11:0.99	.143
7:2.40	8.64	7.20	10.08	5.184	1:11.76	7.20	4.32	9:2.16	1:11.76	11:1.92	.144
7:3.00	8.70	7.25	10.15	5.22	1:11.925	7.25	4.35	9:2.925	1:11.925	11:2.85	.145
7:3.60	8.76	7.30	10.22	5.256	2:0.09	7.30	4.38	9:3.69	2:0.09	11:3.78	.146
7:4.20	8.82	7.35	10.29	5.292	2:0.255	7.35	4.41	9:4.455	2:0.255	11:4.71	.147
7:4.80	8.88	7.40	10.36	5.328	2:0.42	7.40	4.44	9:5.22	2:0.42	11:5.64	.148
7:5.40	8.94	7.45	10.43	5.364	2:0.585	7.45	4.47	9:5.985	2:0.585	11:6.57	.149
7:6.00	9.00	7.50	10.50	5.40	2:0.75	7.50	4.50	9:6.75	2:0.75	11:7.50	.150
7:6.60	9.06	7.55	10.57	5.436	2:0.915	7.55	4.53	9:7.515	2:0.915	11:8.43	.151
7:7.20	9.12	7.60	10.64	5.472	2:1.08	7.60	4.56	9:8.28	2:1.08	11:9.36	.152
7:7.80	9.18	7.65	10.71	5.508	2:1.245	7.65	4.59	9:9.045	2:1.245	11:10.29	.153
Length of Interior Window Casing.				Distance from Floor Line to Top of Window Stool.	Height of Room Base of Skirting.	Height of Window Stool, or Sill.	Height of Exterior Doors.	Distance from Window Soffit to Ceiling.		Clear height of Story.	

TABLE OF COLUMN FINISH.—*Continued.*

Length of Shaft.	Diameter of Shaft above Base.	Diameter of Shaft at Neck.	Height of Capital.	Height of Shaft Base.	Whole height of Pedestal.	Height of Pedestal Base.	Height of Pedestal Cornice.	Distance from Floor Line to Level Line of Entablature.	Height of Entablature.	Whole height of Column.	One Minute.
7:8.40	9.24	7.70	10.78	5.544	2:1.41	7.70	4 62	9:9.81	2:3 11	11:11 22	.151
7:9.00	9 30	7.75	10.85	5.58	2:1.575	7.75	4 65	9:10.575	2:4 575	12:0.15	.155
7:9.60	9.36	7.80	10.92	5.616	2:1.710	7.80	4 68	9:11 31	2:4 710	12:4 08	.156
7:10.20	9.42	7.85	10 99	5 652	2:1.905	7.85	4 71	10:0 105	2:4.905	12:2 01	.157
7:10.80	9.48	7.90	11.05	5.688	2:2.07	7 90	4.74	10:0.87	2:2 07	12:2 94	.158
7:11.40	9.54	7.95	11.11	5.724	2:2.235	7 95	4.77	10:1 635	2:2 235	12:3 87	.159
8:0.00	9.60	8 00	11.20	5.76	2:2 40	8 00	4.80	10:2 40	2:2 40	12:4 80	.160
8:0.60	9.66	8 05	11 27	5.796	2:2.565	8.50	4 83	10:3.165	2:2 565	12:5 73	161
8:1.20	9 72	8.10	11.34	5.832	2:2 73	8 10	4 86	10:3.93	2:2 73	12:6 66	162
8:1.80	9.78	8.15	11.41	5.868	2:2.895	8 15	4 89	10:4 695	2:2.895	12:7 59	163
8:2.40	9.84	8 20	11.48	5.904	2:3.06	8 20	4 92	10:5 46	2:3.06	12:8 52	164
8:3.00	9.90	8 25	11.55	5 94	2:3.225	8.25	4 95	10:6 225	2:3 225	12:9.45	165
8:3.60	9.96	8.30	11.62	5.976	2:3.39	8 30	4 98	10:6 99	2:3 39	12:10.38	166
8:4.20	10.02	8.35	11.69	6.012	2:3.555	8 35	5 01	10:7.755	2:3 555	12:11 31	167
8:4.80	10.08	8.40	11.76	6 018	2:3.72	8 40	5 04	10:8.52	2:3.72	13:0.24	168
8:5.40	10.14	8.45	11.83	6.084	2:3.885	8.45	5.07	10:9 285	2:3 885	13:1.17	169
8:6.00	10.20	8.50	11 90	6.12	2:4 05	8.50	5 10	10:10.05	2:4 05	13:2 10	170
8:6.60	10.26	8.55	11.97	6.156	2:4.215	8.55	5 13	10:10.815	2:4 215	13:3.03	171
8:7.20	10.32	8.60	12.04	6 192	2:4.38	8.60	5.16	10:11.58	2:4 38	13:3.98	172
8:7.80	10.38	8 65	12.11	6.228	2:4.545	8.65	5.19	11:0 345	2:4 545	13:4.89	173
8:8.40	10.44	8.70	12.18	6.264	2:4.71	8.70	5.22	11:1 11	2:4 71	13:5.82	174
8:9.00	10.50	8.75	12.25	6.30	2:4.875	8 75	5.25	11:1.875	2:4.875	13:6 75	175
8:9.60	10.56	8.80	12.32	6.336	2:5.04	8.80	5 28	11:2.64	2:5.04	13:7.68	176
8:10.20	10.62	8 85	12.39	6 372	2:5.205	8.85	5.31	11:3 405	2:5.205	13:8.61	177
8:10.80	10.68	8.90	12.46	6.408	2:5.37	8.90	5 34	11:4 17	2:5.37	13:9.54	178
8:11.40	10.74	8 95	12.53	6.444	2:5.535	8.95	5.37	11:4.935	2:5.535	13:10.47	179
9:0.00	10 80	9.00	12.60	6.48	2:5.70	9 00	5.40	11:5.70	2:5.70	13:11.40	.180
9:0.60	10.86	9.05	12.67	6.516	2:5.865	9.05	5.43	11:6.465	2:5.865	14:0.33	181
9:1.20	10.92	9.10	12.74	6.552	2:6.03	9.10	5.46	11:7 23	2:6.03	14:1 26	182
Length of Interior Window Casing.					Distance from Floor Line to Top of Window Stool.	Height of Room Base or Skirting.	Height of Window Stool or Sill.	Height of Exterior Doors.	Distance from Window Soffit to Ceiling.	Clear height of Story.	

TABLE OF COLUMN FINISH.—*Continued.*

Length of Shaft.	Diameter of Shaft above Base.	Diameter of Shaft at Neck.	Height of Capital.	Height of Shaft Base.	Whole height of Pedestal.	Height of Pedestal Base.	Height of Pedestal Cornice.	Distance from Floor Line to lowest Line of Entablature.	Height of Entablature.	Whole height of Column.	One Minute.
9:1.80	10.98	9.15	12.81	6.588	2:6.195	9.15	5.49	11:7.995	2:6.195	14:2.19	.183
9:2.40	11.04	9.20	12.88	6.624	2:6.36	9.20	5.52	11:8.76	2:6.36	14:3.12	.184
9:3.00	11.10	9.25	12.95	6.66	2:6.525	9.25	5.55	11:9.525	2:6.525	14:4.05	.185
9:3.60	11.16	9.30	13.02	6.696	2:6.69	9.30	5.58	11:10.29	2:6.69	14:4.98	.186
9:4.20	11.22	9.35	13.09	6.732	2:6.855	9.35	5.61	11:11.055	2:6.855	14:5.91	.187
9:4.80	11.28	9.40	13.16	6.768	2:7.02	9.40	5.64	11:11.82	2:7.02	14:6.84	.188
9:5.40	11.34	9.45	13.23	6.804	2:7.185	9.45	5.67	12:0.585	2:7.185	14:7.77	.189
9:6.00	11.40	9.50	13.30	6.84	2:7.35	9.50	5.70	12:1.35	2:7.35	14:8.70	.190
9:6.60	11.46	9.55	13.37	6.876	2:7.515	9.55	5.73	12:2.115	2:7.515	14:9.63	.191
9:7.20	11.52	9.60	13.44	6.912	2:7.68	9.60	5.76	12:2.88	2:7.68	14:10.56	.192
9:7.80	11.58	9.65	13.51	6.948	2:7.845	9.65	5.79	12:3.645	2:7.845	14:11.49	.193
9:8.40	11.64	9.70	13.58	6.984	2:8.01	9.70	5.82	12:4.41	2:8.01	15:0.42	.194
9:9.00	11.70	9.75	13.65	7.02	2:8.175	9.75	5.85	12:5.175	2:8.175	15:1.35	.195
9:9.60	11.76	9.80	13.72	7.056	2:8.34	9.80	5.88	12:5.94	2:8.34	15:2.28	.196
9:10.20	11.82	9.85	13.79	7.092	2:8.505	9.85	5.91	12:6.705	2:8.505	15:3.21	.197
9:10.80	11.88	9.90	13.86	7.128	2:8.67	9.90	5.94	12:7.47	2:8.67	15:4.14	.198
9:11.40	11.94	9.95	13.93	7.164	2:8.835	9.95	5.97	12:8.235	2:8.835	15:5.07	.199
10:0.00	12.00	10.00	14.00	7.20	2:9.00	10.00	6.00	12:9.00	2:9.00	15:6.00	.200

Length of Interior Window Casing.			Distance from Floor Line to Top of Window Stool.	Height of Room Base or Skirting.	Height of Window Stool or Sill.	Height of Exterior Doors.	Distance from Window Sill to Ceiling.	Clear height of Story.

By a careful examination of the foregoing tables, any one at all familiar with designing or building houses can correctly determine the proper height for the window and exterior door openings, the height of the room base, window-stool, stucco cornices, etc. for almost every height of story that could be wanted. When the height of the story has been determined, the exact size of the members of mouldings, etc., can be found by simply multiplying the *number* of minutes contained in any given member by the unit of measure, or minute given in the last column of figures opposite the clear height of the story.

www.ingramcontent.com/pod-product-compliance
Lightning Source LLC
Chambersburg PA
CBHW031249260626
47169CB00007B/2507